CONTENTS

Cole Day lives in the town of Shiverton with his parents, his sister, Winter, and pet dog, Jeff.

All a bit boring until, one day... **COSSSSHHH!** A stray snowball hit Cole on the back of his head!

But it wasn't just any snowball. It was a RADIOACTIVE snowball! And it turned Cole into Snow-Man – the world's chilliest superhero!

Now, whenever he munches on a raw carrot, Cole's body transforms into a big, white, fluffy man of action!

It's down to Snow-Man and his team, **THIN ICE** and **FROSTBITE**, to defeat the world's nastiest weather-changing villains.

Bad guys, you'd better freeze! SNOW-MAN is slip-sliding your way...

CAST OF CHARACTERS

Cole

Winter

Jeff

Chuck Ingit-Down

SNOW-MAN

VOCABULARY

cowered   opportunity

experimenting   shuddered

helicopter   situation

Chapter One

Dry

Cole Day stared down at his maths homework and sighed. He'd only just started back at school after the summer, and his new teacher seemed keen on making his brain hurt at every opportunity.

Mum sat down at the table beside him. "How's it going?" she asked.

"Great!" said Cole. "If you're some kind of alien maths genius. Which I'm not!"

"I wish I could help you," said Mum. "But the only maths I'm good at is working out the temperatures to give out on my TV weather forecast."

"That's OK, Mum," Cole said with a smile. "I'll figure it out somehow."

Mum went back to whatever she was doing on the kitchen counter. "Oh, and I'm pretty good at working out the quantities I need for my new recipe ideas…"

Chapter Two
Damp

Cole hurried out of the kitchen and ran for the front door.

"Don't forget your coat and boots!" Mum called after him. "I predicted heavy rain for today from the weather helicopter this morning!"

Cole grabbed his boots and pulled them on. His mum was the local TV weather presenter and, thankfully, her reports were a lot better than her cooking.

If she said it was going to rain, then that's what would happen. It was already starting to drizzle as Cole hurried outside.

He zipped up his coat and ran down the street towards the shops.

Before long, he spotted his sister, Winter, and their pet dog up ahead.

"Hello, Jeff!" said Cole, patting the pooch on his head as he caught up with them.

His hand came away feeling both damp and sticky. He wiped his palm on his trousers.

The rain started to fall more heavily. Mum's report had been spot on.

"Cole!" said Winter, urgently. "I've been waiting for you to find us. Something is very wrong!"

"I know it is," said Cole. "Mum wants to stick the batter to her fish with honey and toffee! It's her worst recipe idea yet!"

"No, it's not that..."

"Luckily, she can't start cooking until she fixes her favourite kitchen knife," Cole said. "If we pretend the shops didn't have any glue – we'll have to get a takeaway pizza!"

"The shops didn't have any glue," said Winter. "We don't have to pretend."

Cole scowled. "What? Every shop had sold out of glue?"

Winter nodded. "Every single shop. One person went around town buying all the glue this morning."

"Who was that?" asked Cole.

Winter opened her mouth to answer, but Cole stopped her.

"Wait a minute!" he said. "Tell me after I jump into that massive puddle over there!"

"No!" cried Winter. "Wait!"

But Cole didn't wait. He ran over to the huge puddle and jumped right into the middle of it.

But instead of making a cool **SPLASH!** sound, it went **SCHLUPPPPPPP!**

And Cole found he couldn't move.

Chapter Three
Drizzle

"What's going on?" Cole cried from the middle of the puddle. "I'm stuck here!"

"That's what I've been trying to tell you!" said Winter. "The rain is sticky!"

"Sticky rain?" said Cole, looking up at the falling water.

Winter was right – the raindrops were sticking to his cheeks instead of running down his face.

"Jeff and I have been stuck in this puddle for nearly an hour," said Winter.

"But how?" asked Cole. "Who can make the rain sticky like this?"

"It has to be the person who bought all of Shiverton's glue this morning!" said Winter.

"Ooh, she's clever!" said a voice from behind them. "Very clever indeed."

Cole and Winter twisted round in their puddles to see a figure hurrying towards them.

He was a round man, dressed all in blue.

He wore a helmet, and safety pads like those of an ice-hockey player.

"My name is Chuck!" he beamed, carefully jumping over the puddles. "Chuck Ingit-Down!"

Winter pulled her phone out to run a search on the bad guy – but Chuck snatched the gadget from her hands.

"Hey!" she yelled. "That's mine!"

"Not any more, it's not!" grinned Chuck. He dropped the phone into a bag at his side. "Spraying the clouds with glue makes it easy to steal stuff from people!"

Jeff began to growl deep in his throat.

Chuck ignored him and turned to Cole. "Have you got anything I can steal?"

"Not with me," said Cole. "But I can tell you where to find a maths homework book, if you want that…"

"No, thank you!" said Chuck, pulling a face. "I need to keep moving or I'll get stuck too!"

Then he turned and ran away – just as his sticky rain began to hammer down around them.

"I need a carrot!" said Cole, reaching into his pocket.

Chapter Four

Rain

Cole bit into his raw carrot.

Instantly, a frozen whirlwind blew up around the street and wrapped itself around the trio. Icicles flashed, rain showered and snow settled at their feet.

A moment later – exactly where Cole had been – stood a white giant of a figure, dressed in a top hat and red scarf.

He had eyes as black as coal, and what remained of the carrot formed his nose.

This was SNOW-MAN – the world's chilliest superhero!

Standing beside Snow-Man were the two members of his super team – a young girl named Thin Ice, and a still-growling dog known as Frostbite.

Pulling hard, Snow-Man managed to drag his boots out of the sticky puddle, then he hurried over to release his fellow heroes from their own gooey gloop.

"This is a sticky situation!" he said. "We have to find a way to stop Chuck Ingit-Down or Shiverton will be in a fix! If I stay out in this tacky torrent for too long, I won't be able to move."

"We need nail polish remover!" said Thin Ice.

Snow-Man blinked. "But, I'm not wearing any nail polish," he said.

He held his snow-white hands out to prove his point.

Winter shook her head. "There is a chemical in nail polish remover called 'acetate'," she explained. "It's the best thing you can get for unsticking glue."

"Brilliant!" said Snow-Man. "But where can we get enough acetate for this downpour?"

Thin Ice smiled. "Mum always does her nails before her weather reports," she said. "I suspect they'll have lots of nail polish remover at the TV studio."

"Then that's where we're headed!" Snow-Man cried. "To the Snow-Mobile, let's go!"

Thin Ice pulled a wooden sledge from her backpack and both she and Snow-Man climbed aboard.

They threw a rope around Frostbite and he began – ever so slowly - to drag them towards Shiverton town centre.

Chapter Five

Downpour

When they reached the TV studio, Snow-Man and Thin Ice leapt off the sledge and ran inside.

Frostbite staggered in after them, exhausted.

"Look," said Thin Ice, pointing to the screen in reception. "There's Mum, giving another report – and she's got freshly painted fingernails!"

"Then let's check her dressing room for the remover," said Snow-Man, racing off down a corridor.

They quickly found Mum's dressing room.

"Wow!" grinned Thin Ice. "That's the biggest bottle of nail polish remover I've ever seen! It's almost as tall as me!"

"The question is," said Snow-Man, "how do we melt all of Shiverton's stickiness as quickly as possible?"

"*BARK!*" said Frostbite. "*BARK! WOOF! BARK!*"

"Frostbite, you're a genius!" cried Snow-Man. "We'll use the TV station's helicopter!"

Ten minutes later, the heroes were hovering over the town in the TV station's helicopter.

Snow-Man was at the controls and Thin Ice clutched the huge bottle of nail polish remover in her hands.

Frostbite cowered in the back with his paws over his eyes...

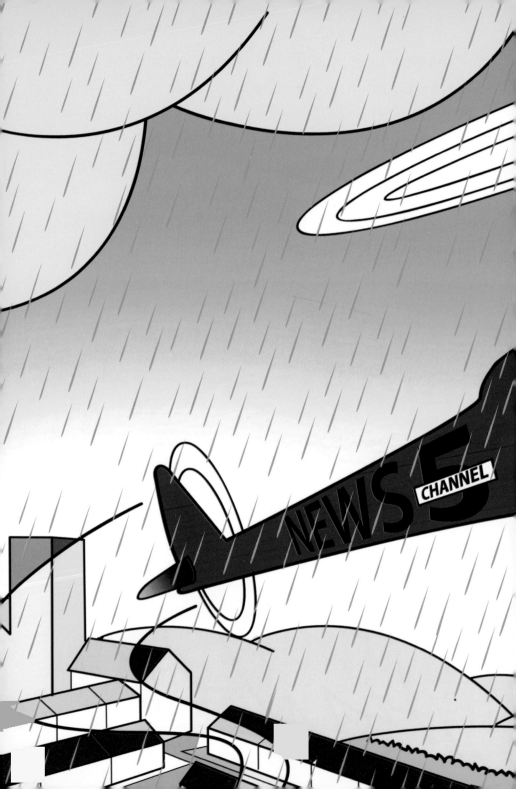

"OK," said Snow-Man over his headset. "Start pouring!"

GLUG!

GLUG!

GLUG!

First, Thin Ice coated all the rainclouds with a fine layer of acetate. "That should stop any more sticky rain from falling!" she said.

Then, Snow-Man flew lower and the team melted the glue keeping everyone trapped in their puddles.

"Now, for the man behind the plan..." he said.

Snow-Man landed the helicopter in front of a very surprised Chuck Ingit-Down.

In fact he was so shocked that he fell backwards and landed in the one puddle that hadn't been treated with the nail polish remover.

"Help!" he cried, trying to free himself. "I can't get up!"

Snow-Man pulled the bad guy free.

Frostbite dragged the bag of stolen stuff from his shoulder, and Thin Ice slipped handcuffs over his wrists.

"What a great team!" declared Snow-Man. "We can do anything if we stick together!"

QUESTIONS

1. What kind of homework was Cole doing? *(page 6)*

2. What was Mum planning to make for tea? *(page 7)*

3. What had sold out in Shiverton? *(page 11)*

4. What did Chuck steal from Winter? *(page 15)*

5. How did Snow-Man get to the TV studio? *(page 20)*

6. Who flew the helicopter? *(page 23)*

MEET THE
AUTHOR AND ILLUSTRATOR

THE AUTHOR

Tommy Donbavand spent his school days writing stories in which more popular kids than him were attacked and devoured by slavering monsters. Years later, he's still doing the same thing – only now people pay him for it. The fools!

THE ILLUSTRATOR

Steve Beckett has a robot arm that is programmed to draw funny pictures. He likes playing with toy soldiers and dreams of being an ace survival expert. He is scared of heights, creepy crawlies and doesn't like camping!